by **JOSH LEWIS**
illustrated by **STEPHEN GILPIN**

𝒟𝒾𝓈𝓃𝑒𝓎 • **HYPERION BOOKS**
NEW YORK

First Edition
1 3 5 7 9 10 8 6 4 2
V567-9638-5-11166

This book is set in 13 point Excelsior.
Printed in the United States of America

Library of Congress Cataloging-in-Publication Data

Lewis, Josh.
 Super Chicken Nugget Boy and the Massive Meatloaf Man manhunt /
by Josh Lewis; [illustrated by Stephen Gilpin].—1st ed.
    p. cm.
 Summary: Gordonville's "best of the breaded," Super Chicken Nugget
Boy, faces his most dreaded adversary yet when Massive Meatloaf Man
emerges from the woods.
 ISBN 978-1-4231-1501-4 (hardcover)
 ISBN 978-1-4231-1536-6 (paperback)
 [1. Superheroes—Fiction. 2. Schools—Fiction. 3. Humorous stories.]
I. Gilpin, Stephen, ill. II. Title.
 PZ7.L5872Sr 2011
 [Fic]—dc22   2011014195

Reinforced binding

Visit www.disneyhyperionbooks.com

SUSTAINABLE FORESTRY INITIATIVE

Certified Fiber Sourcing

www.sfiprogram.org

THIS LABEL APPLIES TO TEXT STOCK

For my nephews Yona and Aytan, who eat more chicken nuggets than anyone I know—J.L.

To all the rugrats in my house. Without them I wouldn't have known enough about massive meatloaves to have done nearly as good a job illustrating this book—S.G.

1

CHICKEN FOOT FIGHT

Karl Nasty Foothead, Gordonville's most famous horrible foot-headed evildoer, sat in his secret hideout counting all the socks that he'd been stealing from unsuspecting Gordonvillites. He needed the socks to use as face-warmers.

Unfortunately for Foothead, his sock celebration was about to go bust!

"Freeze, Foothead!" Super Chicken Nugget Boy demanded as he came bursting through the hideout door. "Stop right there! Those socks are never going to warm your freakish-footed face!"

"Super Chicken Nugget Boy!" cried Nasty Foothead. "How in the world did you ever find me?"

"Please," said Super Chicken Nugget Boy, "I can smell that foot of yours from a mile away. *Pee-yew*."

"I guess Mama Foothead was right," said Karl Nasty. "Always remember to wash your feet."

"That's right, Foothead," said Super Chicken Nugget Boy. "But it's too late for that now, because it's over!"

"Are you kidding me? It's just begun!" said Nasty Foothead, as he unleashed one of his famous shocking sock assaults at Super Chicken Nugget Boy, swiftly picking up dozens of pairs of socks at a time and launching them with all his might at the nug!

"Take that! And that! And that!" he cried,

as he bombarded Super Chicken Nugget Boy with hundreds of socks in a matter of seconds!

The socks, however, did nothing to scare Super Chicken Nugget Boy away. In fact, he was still standing and was still completely fine.

"Wait a second! What's happening?" said Nasty Foothead. "No one is resistant to getting socked by my supersonic assaults! How is it that you are?"

"Well, that's not the only trick I've got up my sleeve," said Karl Nasty. He stuck his foot-head right up in Super Chicken Nugget Boy's face.

"Say hello to my little friends," he said as he wiggled his toes around.

"Oh, how cute," said Super Chicken Nugget Boy. Then . . .

Fwap!

Foothead karate-chopped Super Chicken Nugget Boy right in the face with his index toe!

Super Chicken Nugget Boy stumbled backward.

"Whoa! What an amazingly mighty toe."

"You bet your ankles it's mighty," said Foothead. "Let me introduce you to its little friends."

Foothead wound his middle toe back.

"This little piggy went *slap!*"

Foothead slapped Super Chicken Nugget Boy across the cheek with his middle toe.

"This little piggy went *smack!*"

Foothead hit Super Chicken Nugget Boy in the leg with his fourth toe.

"This little piggy went *whack!*"

Foothead hit Super Chicken Nugget Boy in the gut with his little toe so hard it sent his prize pinkie-toe ring flying.

"And this little piggy went wee, wee, wee, right in your *nose!*"

Foothead wound his big toe back and screamed, *"Raaaaar!"*

Super Chicken Nugget Boy screamed back. *"Urgh! Ug!"*

Foothead swung his mighty toe toward Super Chicken Nugget Boy, but just before he could deliver the knockout thump, Super

Chicken Nugget Boy grabbed Foothead's foot-head and wrapped his arms around it in a foothead headlock.

"Hey, what the . . . ?" said Karl Nasty.

"Say hello to *my* little friends," said Super Chicken Nugget Boy, as he wiggled his fingers in Foothead's face.

"Whoa! What are you doing? What's going on?" cried Foothead.

Super Chicken Nugget Boy reached up and started tickling the bottom of Foothead's toes, which were on top of his head, of course. That was when Foothead freaked, laughing hysterically while begging for mercy.

And then the cops showed up.

"All right, Foothead, you're coming with us," said one of the cops as they cuffed him. But Foothead just kept cracking up. "Ha-ha-ha-ha-ha-ha!"

"I wish all the bad guys thought it was that funny to get hauled off to the slammer," Super Chicken Nugget Boy said to the cops. "It would make my job a whole lot easier."

2
DISPLAY AND RELAY

All of the students at Bert Lahr Elementary School filed into the school auditorium. It was two twenty on a Friday afternoon, which could only mean one thing at Bert Lahr Elementary School—DISPLAY AND RELAY!

Some people said that Display and Relay was just show-and-tell with a different name. But then again, some people said that Paris was just Peoria with a different name, or that *sun* was just another word for a really big flashlight.

Yes, it's true that in Display and Relay

kids show things and yes, it's also true that kids tell things about the things they show, but have you ever heard of anyone bringing their grandpa in to show-and-tell so that he can stretch his neck skin up over his face for the kids? Or have you ever heard of any kid presenting a lump of Benjamin Franklin's cousin's earwax in show-and-tell before? Doubt it. But those are precisely the kinds of things that the kids at Bert Lahr Elementary School brought in for Display and Relay. On top of that, the entire school did Display and Relay together, which meant that the freakier, funkier, or more altogether far-out the thing you brought in was, the cooler the kids in the school thought you were.

Mr. Zwerkle, the music teacher, walked out onto the auditorium stage. He was in charge of Display and Relay.

"Welcome," he said in a booming voice, "to Display and Relay!"

The kids erupted in hoots and hollers and applause!

"WOOOOOOOOO!!!"

"All right," he said, "now, we've got a terrific team of Displayer Relayers for you today, so let's not waste any time. Our first Displayer Relayer is second grader Connie Spicoli! LET'S HEAR IT FOR CONNIE!"

Everyone applauded as the curtains opened to reveal Connie standing in the center of the stage, holding a bag.

She opened the bag and pulled out a long piece of plastic and held it up for everyone to see.

"This is called an Elizabethan collar," said Connie. "It's a piece of plastic that my dad wrapped around our dog Slumpy's neck so that

ice cream cone

slumpy

he couldn't bite or lick or scratch his wounds while they were healing after he had to have doggie ear surgery. It looked like an ice-cream cone when it was wrapped around Slumpy's neck, except that instead of having ice cream on the top of it, it had Slumpy's head at the bottom of it. Thank you."

The students gave Connie a lukewarm round of applause as she headed off the stage. They were not at all impressed.

"That might be cool for show-and-tell,"

Allan Chen said to Roy Clapmist, "but not for Display and Relay!"

"Agreed," said Roy Clapmist. "Agreed."

"All right," said Mr. Zwerkle, "let's keep it moving right along. Next, we have Dirk Hamstone!"

Nobody clapped for Dirk until he stepped from the side of the stage to the center of it and glared at everyone. Then they burst into applause, afraid of what he might do to them if they didn't.

Dirk was carrying a box covered in a black velvet cloth.

He set the box down on a table and stared out at the crowd.

He squinted.

"Nature," he said in a whisper. "It amazes. It alarms. Kill or be killed—that's the rule of the great outdoors. Be warned! What I am about to show you is not for the faint of heart."

He reached down and grabbed the top of the velvet cloth.

"Prepare to be shocked, awed, and astonished," he whispered.

He lifted the cloth and screamed, "Behold!"

Everyone gasped, "Ooh . . . ahh . . ." and then all at once, they burst into thunderous applause.

Dirk smiled a proud little evil smile as he gestured down toward what he had brought— a snake in an aquarium. But not just any snake, no. It was a snake that had recently eaten a porcupine. You could actually see the outline of the porcupine perfectly inside the snake.

"Now that's what Display and Relay is all about!" Roy Clapmist said to Allan Chen.

"You said it!" said Allan.

"My, oh, my," Mr. Zwerkle said to the kids as he walked back to center stage. "Amazing. Thank you, Dirk."

"You're welcome," Dirk said, smiling his proud little evil smile as he grabbed his snake and headed offstage.

"Finally," said Mr. Zwerkle, "we have Fernando Goldberg."

"Oh . . ." Fern said from his seat, surprised.

"I didn't know . . . I mean, I didn't remember . . . I mean, I forgot it was my turn this week."

"What?" said Janice Oglie. "How could you forget?"

"Yeah," said Winnie Kinney. "How could you forget?"

"You can't forget," said Donna Wergnort.

"There's nothing you can display for us?" Mr. Zwerkle asked.

"I'm afraid not," said Fern.

"What a rip-off!" Finneus Washington shouted.

"Yeah!" said Gerard Venvent. "Display and Relay always has three displays! Always!"

"Now, kids," said Mr. Zwerkle, "let's just try to stay calm."

But the kids didn't stay calm. They started chanting. *"One more display! One more display!"*

Mr. Zwerkle didn't know what to do. He looked at Fern.

Fern put his hands in his pockets and scrunched down in his chair, embarrassed.

Just then, he felt something in his pocket, something he'd forgotten he had.

He called out to Mr. Zwerkle. "Mr. Zwerkle! Mr. Zwerkle, I have something."

The kids quieted down.

"Terrific!" said Mr. Zwerkle. "Get up here, and let's see it."

"Oh," said Fern, "I'll just do it from my seat. It's just a little thing."

"Okay," said Mr. Zwerkle, "have it your way."

Fern faced the crowd. "Um . . . well, this is this thing that I, uh . . . well . . . you see . . ."

"Just show it!" shouted Allan Chen.

"Oh, yeah, okay," said Fern.

He reached into his pocket, pulled the thing out, and held it up.

"Oh my God!" shouted Roy Clapmist.

"Is that . . . ?" shouted Janice Oglie.

"It sure is!" said Allan Chen, "I'd recognize it anywhere! That's Karl Nasty Foothead's pinkie-toe ring!"

All the kids burst out screaming and clapping and jumping up and down!

"Wooooo!!! Aaaahhhh!!! Woo hooooo!!!"

"I think that's the coolest thing anyone has ever brought in to Display and Relay!" Allan Chen said to Roy Clapmist.

"It has to be!" Roy said back. "It has to be!"

"How did you get it?" Donna Wergnort asked Fern over the screaming.

"Oh," said Fern, "um . . . Super Chicken Nugget Boy gave it to me."

"That's so cool!" screamed Winnie Kinney.

Meanwhile, as the kids continued to whoop it up well past dismissal time, one kid walked out of the auditorium in a huff.

"That kid really gets my goat," Dirk Hamstone said to his sidekick, Snort, who was right by his side.

"I didn't know you had a goat," said Snort. "Maybe you should've fed your goat to the snake. Maybe that would've worked out better."

"I don't have a goat!" screamed Dirk. "It's an expression, Snortbrain!"

"Oh," said Snort. "Yeah . . . I knew that. *Snort! Snort!*"

"I used to be the king of Display and Relay," said Dirk, "until that kid came to this school. Now look at me . . . I'm nothing but a second-rate Displayer Relayer."

"Aw c'mon, Dirk," said Snort. "Don't be so hard on yourself. Cheer up!"

"Don't tell me to cheer up!" screamed Dirk. "That just makes me madder. Now, let's go . . ."

"Where are we going?" Snort asked.

"Someplace where we can chop things up and throw junk at living stuff," said Dirk.

"Good idea," said Snort, as they headed out. "That'll cheer you up!"

"WHAT DID I JUST SAY?" Dirk yelled.

3

YOU NEVER KNOW WHAT'S BURKING AROUND THE CORNER

"hat was totally awesome in there," Lester said to Fern as they walked home. "People are going to be talking about that Display and Relay for the rest of their lives!"

"Hmm," sighed Fern.

"How could you forget that you had Foothead's pinkie-toe ring in your pocket?"

"I guess it just slipped my mind," said Fern, and then he sighed again. "Hmm."

"What's up?" Lester asked.

Fern shook his head. "I don't know. I mean, don't get me wrong, I love fighting crime and being a superhero who's a giant version of a food that everyone loves to eat and everything, but I mean, I guess it's just . . . well, sometimes it gets exhausting; you know what I mean?"

"No, not exactly," said Lester. "I mean, I'm not a Super Chicken Nugget Boy or anything."

"Good point," said Fern. "Well, I guess all I'm saying is it's been a pretty busy crime-fighting season."

"That's for sure," said Lester. "First, there was Dandruff Dan, then there was Genie in the Bottle, who looked so cute and harmless until she smashed people over the head with her bottle. And we can't forget Ward the Window Washer. And then there was Flower Boy, and Rocks Inhishead, and, oh, of course, the Spatula. . . ."

"Yeah," said Fern, "and that's all just this month."

"I think I see what you mean now," said Lester.

"You do?" asked Fern.

"Yeah," said Lester, "and I've got just what the doctor ordered."

In less than an hour, Fern and Lester found themselves in the Burkeburke Hills, high above Gordonville.

"This was a great idea," Fern said to Lester as they hiked up toward their campsite.

"Yup," said Lester. "Nothing like the great outdoors to get the ol' batteries recharged."

"Ain't that the truth," said Fern. "And best of all, it's just us."

"You and me and no one else," said Lester.

"No one to bug us and keep us from having a good time," said Fern.

"No bad guys!" said Lester.

"No guys at all!" said Fern.

"HALLELUJAH!" shouted Lester.

Just then they heard something off in the distance. It was a revving sound.

"What do you think that noise is?" Lester asked.

"Who knows?" said Fern. "The only thing I know is that it isn't going to get in the way of my having a nice, relaxing weekend."

The revving sound got really loud, and then a MAPURV (Mini All-Purpose Ultra-Rugged Vehicle) came racing around the corner, kicking up the dirt as it sped right toward Fern and Lester.

Lester frowned. "Great," he said, shaking his head. "Just great."

Sure enough, behind the wheel of the MAPURV was Dirk Hamstone, with his trusty snorty sidekick seated next to him.

"What are *they* doing here?" Lester asked.

"I don't know, and I don't care," said Fern. "But the Burkeburkes are big enough for all of us and I'm not about to let those two ruin our retreat."

"Yeah," said Lester.

Dirk pulled his MAPURV right up next to Fern and Lester and screeched on the brakes.

"What are you two losers doing up here?" Dirk asked them.

"Yeah," said Snort. "*Snort!* Losers! *Snort!*"

"We were just about to ask you the same question," said Fern.

"Well," said Dirk, "if you must know, I'll tell you. . . . Mind your own business!"

"That's exactly why we're up here, too," said Fern.

"All right then!" said Dirk. "Fine."

"Fine," said Fern.

"Fine. *Snort!*" said Snort.

"Fine. *Snort!*" said Lester.

Dirk slammed his foot on the gas and took off, moving up higher into the hills.

Fern looked at Lester. "Did you just snort at them?" he asked.

"Yeah," said Lester, "I guess I did. That was weird."

4
FOREST MIRE

Fern and Lester set up their camp deep inside the forest, near the top of the Burkeburkes.

"Perfect," said Fern, as he finished hammering the final tent stake into the ground. "Now, I don't know about you, but I'm ready to hit Burkeburke Brook."

"Heck yeah! Heckety-heck-heck-yeah," said Lester as they left their campsite and headed off for a dip.

The refreshing water of Burkeburke Brook hit the spot. Fern forgot all about the fact that he was the world's number one chicken nugget superhero. For the moment, he was just a simple boy, without a care in the world. . . . That is, until he and Lester got out of the water.

If you've ever been to the Burkeburke Hills and swum in Burkeburke Brook, you know how cold it is when you get out and that Burkeburke breeze starts blowing against your bare body. That's exactly when a shirt or a towel, or hopefully both, comes in handy. If you don't have a towel or a shirt, well, then, your name is Fern or Lester, and you're *unbelievably miserable*! Their shirts and towels and shoes were all missing!

Fern and Lester made their way back to camp, shivering all the way, along the rocky Burkeburke Trail, each barefooted step more painful than the last.

That wasn't the only trouble Fern and Lester ran into that night.

Fern and Lester were completely worn out by the time they hit the sack.

They laid their heads down on their sleeping bags.

"Well," said Fern, "I know things have been a little crazy today, but I have to say I'm still happy we came out here. Sure, there were some setbacks, some uninvited guests playing pitiful pranks, but none of them compared to battling horrendously hideous evildoers. Heck, next to fighting Nasty Foothead, eating a fake doggie hot dog sounds pretty good. Wouldn't you say, Lester? . . . Lester?"

Lester didn't answer.

"Hey, Lester, you asleep already?"

Still no answer.

"Huh," said Fern. "That's too bad. I thought we'd get in at least one good ghost story before we nodded off. Oh, well. Good night, Les."

Fern closed his eyes, but the second he did . . .

"HELLLLLPPP!!!"

It was Lester calling out to him.

"What?" Fern said, as he jumped out of his sleeping bag and bolted over to Lester's.

Lester wasn't there! Neither was his sleeping bag!

"Where are you?" Fern cried.

"Over here!" yelled Lester.

"Where's over here?" said Fern.

"I don't know," Lester yelled back. "Follow my voice!"

"But your voice keeps moving," yelled Fern.

"That's because I'm moving!" said Lester.

"Why?" Fern asked.

"It wasn't my idea!" said Lester. "I'm being carried away! AAAHHH!!!"

Fern started to run in the direction of Lester's voice.

"BY WHO?" Fern asked.

"I CAN'T TELL! IT'S TOO DARK!" Lester answered.

Fern didn't know why he was bothering to ask. He was sure who was behind this stunt.

"JUST BREAK FREE!" Fern shouted.

"I CAN'T!" said Lester. "MY BODY'S TRAPPED INSIDE MY SLEEPING BAG!"

"LISTEN HERE, DIRK AND SNORT!" Fern shouted, "THIS HAS GONE FAR ENOUGH! LET HIM GO RIGHT NOW!"

There was no answer.

"DID YOU HEAR ME, DIRK?" Fern shouted again.

"THEY'RE NOT LETTING GO!" Lester yelled back.

"ALL RIGHT, WELL, DON'T WORRY! I'M COMING AFTER YOU! JUST DON'T STOP TALKING. IT'S THE ONLY WAY I KNOW WHERE YOU ARE," said Fern.

"NOT A PROBLEM!" said Lester, "IT'S ONE OF MY FAVORITE THINGS TO DO!"

Fern chased after Lester down the Berryburke Trail.

"CAN YOU STILL HEAR MY VOICE?" Lester shouted.

"YUP!" answered Fern.

Fern then followed him across Willieburke Ridge.

"I'M STILL TALKING," said Lester. "TALKING, TALKING, TALKING!"

"GOTCHA!" said Fern.

Fern sped after him through the Franklinburke Ferns.

"I DON'T KNOW WHAT ELSE TO SAY," said Lester. "HUM-DI-DEE-DUM! I GUESS I COULD TELL YOU ABOUT THE TIME THAT I SNEEZED SO HARD I THOUGHT I BROKE MY KIDNEYS!"

"FINE," said Fern, running after him. "WHATEVER!"

The chase continued on and on through the Burkeburkes, with Fern chasing after the sound of Lester's voice as Lester told him how the sneeze rumbled through his body, until they reached the very bottom of the hills. That's when Lester stopped telling his story.

"HEY! WHOA! WHAT THE—!" he shouted. "WH— . . . WHAT IN THE NAME OF . . . WHERE ARE YOU PUTTING ME?"

Just then Fern came running up to Lester, who was lying on the ground in his sleeping bag.

"What's going on?" said Fern. "Are you okay?"

"Yeah," said Lester, "I think so . . . I mean . . . uh . . . yeah . . . I just . . ."

"I guess they got away, huh?" Fern said.

"Who?" Lester asked.

"What do you mean, who?" said Fern. "Dirk and Snort."

"Oh, yeah, um, I guess so," said Lester.

5

THE LEGEND OF THE LOAF

So, what do you do when you find yourself stuck at the bottom of the Burkeburkes in the middle of the night?

Good question.

Fortunately—or unfortunately for Fern and Lester—that question was answered for them when a grizzled old man with a walking stick happened to be strolling by just after their chase came to its end.

"You boys all right?" asked the old man.

"Yeah, we're fine," said Fern, "thank you."

"You don't want to be wandering unawares 'round these parts this time o' night. Not with him out there."

"Who?" Lester asked.

"Mameama," said the old man.

"Who's Mameama?" asked Fern.

"Who's Mameama?" said the old man. "He is the hunter and the hunted."

"What does that mean?" asked Lester.

"He is the prisoner and the guard of the Burkeburkes," said the old man.

"What?" Fern asked.

"He is rare, yet he is well-done," said the old man. "Come. I will take you to safety."

The old man brought Fern and Lester to the shed where he lived. It was filled with artifacts—plates and bowls and silverware

and statues and jewelry, all including the
same image—a large gorillalike figure.

"What's with all this stuff?" Fern asked.

"It's Mameama," said the old man.

"Mameama's a gorilla?" said Fern.

"Ha!" said the old man. "Gorillas are simple, gorillas are common. Mameama is one in a million. Have you ever heard of Massive Meatloaf Man?"

"Massive Meatloaf Man?" Fern and Lester repeated in unison.

"Yes. What we who live on the mountain call Mameama, others call Massive Meatloaf Man."

"Never heard of him," said Fern.

The old man went on to tell Fern and Lester all about the history of Massive Meatloaf Man, or Mameama. He told them how for as long as people had been living on and around the Burkeburkes, they'd been talking, singing, and making art for and about Mameama— which explained all the grizzled old man's artifacts. He collected them.

He told them that the ancient natives, many of whom were responsible for the very artifacts Fern and Lester were looking at, believed that Mameama protected them from the dangers of the outside world. In addition, they believed that whoever managed to catch a glimpse of Mameama would have good luck for the rest of their days.

He told them how there were actual historically recorded sightings of Massive Meatloaf Man dating back to 1813, when a gold digger named Angus "Ricketty" Wilmore wrote about seeing an "enormous mad meaty monkey" when he was out digging for gold up in the Burkeburkes. Since that time, the grizzled old man said, hundreds of sightings of the humongous meaty man had been reported in the Burkeburkes every year, and although no one had ever managed to take a close-up picture of Mameama, many people had taken pictures of him from off in the distance, and there were countless close-up photos of his massive meaty tracks as well.

The grizzled old man showed Fern and Lester his collection of pictures.

"These prove nothing," said Fern. "You can't see anything in them."

"That's because you don't *want* to see anything in them," said the old man. "More importantly, *Mameama* doesn't want you to see anything in them."

"I don't buy it," said Fern.

"What about these?" Lester asked Fern, pointing to some pictures of enormous animal (or Mameama) tracks. "They look pretty real to me."

"Are you kidding me?" said Fern. "Those are from a bear."

"No bear is that big," said Lester. "Besides, bears don't have meaty paws."

"Maybe it just finished eating something," said Fern.

"Yeah," said Lester, giving in. "I guess you're right."

"Of course I'm right," said Fern.

"You couldn't be any more wrong," said the old man. "But that's okay; the fewer believers, the better."

"Why?" Lester asked.

"Because all Mameama wants is to be left alone," said the old man. "And when he isn't left alone, he turns raving mad. And when he's raving mad, we all suffer. Things are destroyed, and people are hurt, and the hills quake with fear."

"Okay," said Fern, "thanks for the tip. Now, if you'll excuse us, we have to be going."

"Of course," said the grizzled old man, "go. Go quietly, go safely, and if you smell meat, go in the other direction."

"Sure thing," said Fern. "See you later."

"I hope so," said the old man. "I hope so."

Fern and Lester walked out of the grizzled old man's shed. The sun was starting to come up.

"Boy, what a nut job," said Fern.

"Yeah," said Lester. "Nutty, nut, nut job!"

6

THE MEATLIZATION

It was Monday morning recess. Fern and Lester and Allan Chen and Roy Clapmist were playing Help, I'm Being Eaten by a Shark.

It was Roy's turn to pretend he was being eaten by a shark. He dived into the imaginary water and started stroking with his arms as though he were swimming farther and farther away from the other guys.

"Gosh, oh, golly," said Roy, "what a lovely day for a swim. I could stay out here for . . ."

His body jerked.

"What the—?" Then he was still. . . .

"Oh, I guess it was noth—" His body shook.

"Yikes! Hey, what's down there?"

His body quaked like crazy!

"This is terrible," Lester said to Fern and Allan. "My Help, I'm Being Eaten by a Shark is a million times better."

"AAGHH!!!" Roy screamed. "AAGHH!! Somebody, please h—"

He ducked his head down and flung his arms up above it.

"Glug, glug, glug."

He jerked his head up again.

"I can't . . ."

"This has to be the worst Help, I'm Being Eaten by a Shark I've ever seen," Lester said to the others.

Roy ducked his head back down and shook himself.

He popped his head up and flung his arms all around like a madman.

"AAGHH! Help! I'm being eaten by a sh—"

Roy was planning on saying "shark," and he would've if he hadn't been distracted by Dirk Hamstone, who had strolled over to Fern to start some trouble.

Dirk got right up in Fern's face. "What's your problem?" Dirk asked.

"Yeah," said Snort, who of course was right next to him. *"Snort! Snort!"*

"What are you talking about?" said Fern.

"You know exactly what I'm talking about," said Dirk.

"If I knew exactly what you were talking about, I wouldn't have said, 'What are you talking about?'" said Fern.

"I'm talking about the Burkeburkes," said Dirk.

"Oh, the Burkeburkes," said Fern. "You mean, the place where you guys took our shirts and shoes and towels while we were swimming in Burkeburke Brook?"

"Oh yeah, that was funny," said Dirk.

"Yeah, *snort!*" said Snort.

"I mean, what are you talking about?" said Dirk. "We don't know anything about your shirts and shoes and towels."

"Oh, no?" said Fern.

"No," said Dirk.

"Right," said Fern, "and I suppose you don't know anything about our campsite ending up in a tree."

"Ha-ha-ha. I forgot about that one," said Dirk.

"So, you admit you did it," said Fern.

"No," said Dirk.

"You just said you forgot about that one," said Fern.

"Yeah," said Dirk. "I forgot about that one because I never knew about it."

"Sure," Fern said, "just like you don't know about our hot dogs being replaced by fake doggie dogs!"

Snort cracked up. "*Snort! Snort! Snort!* Oh no, we know about that one, all right. Don't we, Dirk?"

"Shh!" said Dirk. "Of course we don't."

"No, of course not," said Fern, "the same way you don't know anything about Lester getting snatched up and dragged all across the Burkeburkes while I ran after him."

"That's not funny!" Dirk yelled.

"I know it's not funny," said Fern. "That's why you shouldn't have done it."

"I didn't do it!" Dirk yelled.

"Oh, well, that's why Snort shouldn't have done it," said Fern.

"I didn't do it," said Snort.

"Okay—so then, who did it?" Fern asked.

"You did it to me!" Dirk shouted.

"That's ridiculous," said Fern. "Why would I bother doing that to you? I have better things to do with my time."

"Well, somebody did it to Dirk," said Snort.

"Yeah!" said Dirk.

"And somebody did it to Lester," said Fern.

"Yeah!" said Lester.

"And if it wasn't any of us . . ." said Dirk.

"Then who was it?" said Fern.

There was a pause.

"It was Mameama," said Lester.

"What?" Dirk said.

"Massive Meatloaf Man," said Lester.

Everyone was silent.

There was nothing left to be said.

7
LEWIS AND CLARK'S LATEST DISCOVERY

Unfortunately, recess ended before anyone had a chance to dig any deeper into the Massive Meatloaf Mystery. Everyone was back in class, but there were many meatloaf matters still to mull over. Fern and Lester, unable to discuss their views out loud due to Ms. Durbindin's lesson about the great American explorers Lewis and Clark and their epic expedition across North America, used the handout Ms. Durbindin passed around to write notes back and forth to each other.

8

MISSION: MEATLOAF

That night, Dirk's dad, Principal Hamstone, made his world-famous weenie toasties for dinner. Dirk loved weenie toasties and always told his dad to make them.

Dirk wanted nothing to do with weenie toasties that night. He was all about the meat-loaf.

"What do you mean, you want meatloaf?" Principal Hamstone asked.

"Yes," said Mrs. Hamstone, looking at his plate. "These are your favorites, remember?"

"Not anymore," said Dirk. "I WANT MEATLOAF!"

"Well, that's what I made," said Principal Hamstone.

"You don't understand. I have to have meatloaf," said Dirk.

"Why?" Mrs. Hamstone asked.

"To get the taste of it in my mouth," said Dirk.

"To get the taste of it in your mouth?" Mrs. Hamstone repeated.

"Yes," Dirk said, "to make it easier to track him."

"What?" Mrs. Hamstone said.

"To know how he smells. To know how he tastes. To know how he thinks and feels," said Dirk.

"Who?" Mrs. Hamstone asked.

"Who else?" Dirk said. "Massive Meatloaf Man, of course."

"Massive Meatloaf Man?" grumbled

Principal Hamstone, clearly not believing Dirk.

"Yes," said Dirk. "He's the most feared meaty man in all the world, and soon he will be *mine!* Ha-ha-ha! You'll see." Dirk was getting crazier and crazier by the second. "He lives in the forest up in the Burkeburkes. I'm going up there and I'm not coming back until I bring him down with me. Ha-ha-ha! And then do you know what I'm going to do?"

"No," said Mrs. Hamstone.

"I'm going to put him on display," said Dirk.

"What?" said Principal Hamstone.

"You heard me," said Dirk. "I'm going to put him in Display and Relay. And all the students are going to come, and they're going to see him, and they're not going to believe their eyes." Dirk stood up. "They're going to be fascinated and afraid. They're going to want to turn away from the scary beast, but they're not going to be able to because he'll be too mesmerizing! Ha-ha-ha! And everyone will say, 'This was

the greatest Display and Relay of all time,' and it will all be because of ME!" Dirk stood up on his chair. "And no one will ever want to display anything ever again after that, because they'll never be able to top it!" Dirk stood up on the table. *"And I will go down in the history books as the greatest Displayer Relayer of all time! Ha-ha-ha! And that is why I must have meatloaf tonight!"*

"Goodness," said Mrs. Hamstone. "Well, we better get you some right away. Murkwood! Make your son meatloaf!"

"You can't be serious, dear," said Principal Hamstone.

"I've never been more serious in my life," said Mrs. Hamstone. "You heard the boy."

"But, dear . . ." said Principal Hamstone.

Mrs. Hamstone opened her mouth and out it came, just like every other time Principal

Hamstone ever tried to stand up to her. "MURRRRKWOOOOOD!" she screamed, at the top of her lungs.

Principal Hamstone hung his head and trudged over to the refrigerator.

"Yes, dear," he said. "Whatever you say."

He pulled out a package of ground beef.

"That's more like it," said Mrs. Hamstone. She turned to Dirk. "Don't worry, precious, that pesky meaty monster will be yours in no time."

"Ha-ha-ha!" They laughed together, as Principal Hamstone shook his head and squished the ground beef up with his hands.

And now, please welcome Bert Lahr Elementary School music teacher, Harvey Zwerkle.

"REMEMBER: THIS IS A SING-ALONG. YOU HAVE TO SING, OR I'LL GET MY DAD TO GIVE YOU DETENTION!

"Okay, and five, six, seven, eight!"

OH, YEAH, I'LL TELL YOU SOMETHING
YOU WILL NOT UNDERSTAND,
WHEN I SAY THAT SOMETHING—
I WANT A MEATLOAF MAN

I WANT A MEATLOAF MAN.
I WANT A MEATLOAF MAN.

NOW, YOU SAY TO ME
YOU KNOW THAT I'M THE MAN,
AND YOU SAY TO ME
I'LL GET A MEATLOAF MAN.

I NEED A MEATLOAF MAN.
I WANT A MEATLOAF MAN.

AND WHEN I CATCH HIM I'LL FEEL HAPPY, INSIDE
I'LL BE THE COOLEST
GUY THERE IS
THE WORLD WIDE
THE WORLD WIDE
THE WORLD WIDE

YEAH, YOU AIN'T GOT NOTHING
I NEED TO UNDERSTAND
'CUZ I GOT THAT SOMETHING
TO CATCH A MEATLOAF MAN!
I WANT A MEATLOAF MAN.
I WANT A MEATLOAF MAN.
I WANT A MEATLOAF MA-A-A-A-A-AN.

9

FIELD TRAP

If there was one thing Fern loved, it was Ms. Durbindin's Things I Know That You Think I Don't Know trivia contest. That's the game where students pick categories for other students that they think they know nothing about and ask them questions from those categories. Nobody's very good at it because they almost never know anything about the categories, obviously, but that didn't matter to Fern. He just liked the challenge of it. And that day he was doing really well. He got the question: What can help keep you from crying when you're peeling onions? The answer: Chewing gum. And he also knew that your heart beats 100,000 times a day and that mosquitoes don't bite—they suck.

Needless to say, Fern was upset when Ms. Durbindin announced that it was time to stop playing. But not nearly as upset as he was when she told the class that they would be studying the last section of their "Berries You Should Not Eat" unit outdoors, up in the Burkeburkes.

"Um . . ." Fern said, right after she announced it, ". . . can't we just stay here in class and look at the pictures?"

All of Fern's classmates booed, even Lester, who didn't understand Fern's reasoning for wanting to stay in school.

"Are you serious, Fernando?" asked Ms. Durbindin. "You can't tell me that you'd really rather be cooped up in this stuffy class-room than be out in the clean, fresh air."

"I'm totally serious," said Fern. "I don't think the outdoors is a proper environment for serious study."

Fern's classmates booed again, even harder this time.

"BOO!!!"

"What's your problem?" shouted Roy Clapmist.

"Do you even have a soul?" yelled Janice Oglie.

"I disagree," Ms. Durbindin said to Fern. "I think it's a perfect place for study. Especially the study of Berries You Should Not Eat."

"Well, then, can we at least go somewhere

besides the Burkeburkes? It's so boring up there," said Fern.

He did all he could to try to convince Ms. Durbindin to stay away from the Burkeburkes. The last thing he wanted was for his entire class to be eaten by Massive Meatloaf Man. His attempts, unfortunately, were fruitless. Five minutes later, he was heading up into the Burkeburkes with Ms. Durbindin and his class, who all hated his guts now for trying to keep them indoors.

The class had been up in the Burkeburkes for about an hour and forty minutes when Ms. Durbindin spotted something in a clearing that made her eyes light up.

"Ooh!" she said to the class, as she scurried over to a shrub with soft, bright, green needles and soft red berries with hard green centers. "This is very exciting! Gather round. Now, can anyone tell me what this is called?"

"Pokeweed?" Donna Wergnort said.

"Nope," said Ms. Durbindin, "Not poke-weed. Anyone else?"

Fern knew what it was called, but he was too busy trying to keep Arnie Simpson the Salamander in his pocket to answer. He had brought Arnie along just in case, but Arnie had missed his daily afternoon snack because they were having class outside, and so he kept trying to sneak out to eat all of the things the class was coming across.

Ms. Durbindin waited for a moment, but nobody said anything, so she just told them. "This is yew."

"Ooh," said all of the students, impressed.

"Now, who can tell me what will happen if you eat these berries?"

"I can," said Roy Clapmist. "They will cause vomiting, stomach pain, dizziness, difficulty breathing, and some other stuff I can't remember."

"Very good," said Ms. Durbindin.

"I was going to say that," said Lester.

"Ooh!" said Ms. Durbindin, as she spotted another bush a few feet away and started to scamper toward it. "I can't believe our luck! It's a—"

"*AAAARRRRGGGGHHHH!!!*" An earth-shattering roar echoed throughout the Burkeburkes.

"*AAAAAAAHHHHHHH!!!*" screamed the children.

"Oh, my," said Ms. Durbindin.

"What was that?" Janice Oglie asked.

"Well, I don't know," said Ms. Durbindin. "Maybe it was thunder."

Fern and Lester looked at each other. They

knew exactly what it was.

Then it happened again, only this time even louder. "*AAAAARRRRRGGGGGHHHHH!!!*"

"That was not thunder!" said Allan Chen.

"No, I guess not," Ms. Durbindin said.

"What do we do?" Winnie Kinney called out.

"Well, let me see," said Ms. Durbindin, "um . . ."

Then they heard it once again: "*AAAAARRRRRGGGGGHHHHH!!!*"

"*Run!*" Fern yelled, knowing what was about to rear its meaty head.

Everyone screamed, "*AAAAAGHHHHHH!!!*" and started running away from the noise.

"Yes," said Ms. Durbindin, starting to run herself. "That sounds like the right thing to do."

But as soon as she took one step . . .

SNAP!

Her foot got caught in a trap made of rope that snatched her up in a net, sent her soaring twenty feet high, and left her hanging from a tree.

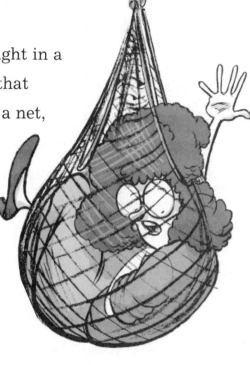

The students all screamed, *"AAAAAAAG- HHHHHHH!!!"*

"Don't worry class, I'll be fine. Save yourselves!" said Ms. Durbindin, as she hung in the giant net.

"We can't just leave her there," Roy Clapmist said.

"AAAAARRRRRGGGGGHHHHH!!!"

"On second thought . . ." said Roy.

All the students nodded and started running again.

"That's right," Ms. Durbindin called to them, "I'll find a way out of here, don't you fret. But in case I don't, can one of you call 911? Oh, and while you're at it, could you phone my family and tell them that I love them . . . just in case."

Fern immediately broke off from the rest of the class when they weren't looking and ran back toward Ms. Durbindin.

"What are you doing?" Lester asked, following behind him.

"Going back to save Ms. Durbindin," said Fern. "What else?"

"Oh, yeah," Lester said. "I was just confused because you said 'run' before."

"Yeah," Fern said, "I told everyone else to

run because they're not superheroes who can save Ms. Durbindin."

"Sure, sure," said Lester. "Sometimes, I just get confused. Sorry."

"It's okay," said Fern.

Just then, none other than Dirk Hamstone and Snort appeared from the opposite side of the clearing.

"Wait!" Fern whispered to Lester, as he pulled him down behind a bush. "Let's see what these two are up to."

After observing things for a few moments, Fern said to Lester, "I should've known he was behind this."

"He's mine! He's mine!" said Dirk.

"He's yours! He's yours!" said Snort.

"Oh, hello, Dirkwood," Ms. Durbindin said from above them.

Dirk looked up at the net.

"RATS!" he said when he saw Ms. Durbindin.

"What are you doing up here?" she asked. "Shouldn't you be in school?"

"No," Dirk said. "I'm excused today."

Dirk was telling the truth. He had dropped off a note that morning for his teacher excusing him from school.

Please excuse Dirkwood
and his friend Snort
from school today.
They need to capture
a Massive Meatloaf
Man up in the
Burkburke Hills.
        Sincerely,
        Mrs. Hamstone
        (Principal Hamstone's
        wife, in case you
        didn't know)

"Well, you probably shouldn't be here, Dirkwood," Ms. Durbindin said. "There's some sort of wild beast roaming around, and he doesn't sound happy. If I were you, I'd get out of here as quickly as I could."

"Are you kidding me?" said Dirk. "That's the reason I am here! I'm going to catch that beast in that very net you're stuck in."

"Sounds like a perfectly insane idea if you ask me, but I'm not going to stand in your way," said Ms. Durbindin.

"Good," said Dirk. "Now, all I have to do is get you down from there."

"Terrific," said Ms. Durbindin.

"All right, Snort," said Dirk. "Go release the pulleys."

"Sure thing!" said Snort. *"Snort!"*

But before Snort could do anything, another *"AAAAARRRRRGGGGGHHHHH!!!"* was heard, along with the thunderous stomping of feet.

Snort froze.

"Oh, my!" said Ms. Durbindin.

"Oh, no!" said Fern.

There was then another *"AAAAARRRRR-GGGGGHHHHH!!!"* as the stomping sound grew louder, and the earth shook!

"Do it!" Dirk yelled at a stunned Snort, but it was too late. At the other end of the clearing stood the one and only most monstrous menace, Massive Meatloaf Man! He bellowed and beat his chest, as Snort snapped out of it and he and Dirk ran for cover.

"YYYYYYYAAAAAAAAAAAAHHHHH!!!" screamed Ms. Durbindin.

Massive Meatloaf Man turned toward the scream, beat his chest some more, and headed over to Ms. Durbindin.

"AAARRRGGGHHH! AAARRRGGGHHH! AAARRRGGGHHH!"

"Amazing!" Dirk said to Snort, from their hiding place behind a rock. "He's the mightiest meat man I've ever seen."

"He's the only meat man I've ever seen," said Snort.

"Shh!" said Dirk.

"Quick!" Fern said to Lester. "Ketchup!"

"I'm getting it," Lester said, as he fumbled around, checking all his pockets for it.

Massive Meatloaf Man arrived, ferociously growling and snarling, at the tree from which Ms. Durbindin's net was hanging. *"AAAARRRRGGGGHHHH!!!"*

"STAY AWAY FROM ME, YOU OVER-GROWN MEAT MONSTER!!!" screamed Ms. Durbindin.

Massive Meatloaf Man screamed again and then looked down at Ms. Durbindin. It was a long, intense look. He had never seen anyone quite like her.

"WHAT ARE YOU LOOKING AT, YOU MAMMOTH MOUNTAIN OF GROSS

GROUND BEEF?" she screamed.

Suddenly Massive Meatloaf Man's mood changed completely. He went from vicious and violent to quiet and shy in an instant.

He put his face right up to the net and stared at Ms. Durbindin.

"STOP LOOKING AT ME LIKE THAT!" she shouted.

But Massive Meatloaf Man didn't stop looking at Ms. Durbindin like that. He was too fascinated . . . some might even say too in love.

Ms. Durbindin's screams didn't bother Massive Meatloaf Man in the least.

He gently lifted up one finger.

"Don't you dare touch me!" Ms. Durbindin yelled. "I know kung fu, karate, judo, jujitsu, and the African-Brazilian martial art and dance form known as capoeira!"

Massive Meatloaf Man poked his finger in through the net.

"AAAGHHH!" screamed Ms. Durbindin as she opened her mouth and bit down on Massive Meatloaf Man's finger!

"AAAARRRRGGGGHHHH!!!" he cried.

"GRRRRRR!" growled Ms. Durbindin as she ripped the tip of Massive Meatloaf Man's finger off with her mouth, then chewed it up and swallowed it down.

"Mmm . . ." she said to herself, quietly, "really quite tasty."

"AAAARRRRGGGGHHHH!!!" Massive Meatloaf Man screamed again and lifted his arms above his head.

"Uh-oh," said Ms. Durbindin.

Massive Meatloaf Man jumped up and down furiously.

"Maybe I shouldn't have done that," said Ms. Durbindin.

Massive Meatloaf Man reached in to grab Ms. Durbindin, this time not gently.

She screamed, "YYYYAAAAAAAAAAAA-HHHHH!!!"

"Finally! I found some!" Lester screamed, as he held up a packet of ketchup.

"Just in the nick of time!" said Fern.

Lester aimed the ketchup at Fern's chest and squeezed.

Squirt!

At the exact same moment, Arnie Simpson the Salamander, smelling the ketchup, sprung out of Fern's pocket and climbed up his stomach.

Splat!

Suddenly, *KERBLAM!* Arnie was transformed into that greatest of great shining slimy soldiers, Arnie the Awesome Amphibian!

Fern, however, was still just plain Fern.

"What happened?" Fern asked Lester.

"I don't know," Lester said. "I guess all the ketchup landed right on Arnie, and absolutely none of it got on you."

"Okay, hit me with another packet," Fern said, as Massive Meatloaf Man turned away from Ms. Durbindin once he spotted Arnie, because Arnie obviously was way too big to get away with hiding in the bushes anymore.

"Um," said Lester, "no can do."

"What do you mean?" Fern asked.

"That was all I had," said Lester.

"You only had one packet?" shouted Fern.

"Yeah," said Lester. "How was I supposed to know that we were going to run into Massive Meatloaf Man and that he'd be so unbelievably massive, and then Arnie would hog all the ketchup? I'm sorry. I do the best I can."

Massive Meatloaf Man stomped over toward Arnie as Fern, Lester, Dirk, and Snort all watched from their hiding places, and Ms. Durbindin watched from inside the net.

10
CLASH OF THE COLOSSAL FREAKS OF NATURE

"Unbelievable!" Dirk said, looking over the meatloaf man. "He's the greatest hunk of flesh there's ever been. And he's going to be mine! Ha-ha-ha! ALL MINE!"

11

NUGGET BOY BACKUP

Arnie tried to get up, but the impact from smashing into Massive Meatloaf's meathead left him too weak and woozy. He only managed to lift his own head a little before it came crashing back down to the ground.

He was out.

Lester, overcome with sadness, screamed, "NO-O-O-O-O-O-O-O-O-O-O-O-O-O-O-O-O!!!"

But then immediately realized what a bad idea that was.

"That was a bad idea, wasn't it?" Lester said to Fern.

"Yes, very bad," said Fern.

Massive Meatloaf Man screamed, *"AAAARRRRGGGGHHHH!!!"* and stomped toward Fern and Lester's hiding place.

As Fern and Lester jumped up to make a break for it, a packet of ketchup fell to the ground. "Whoa!" said Lester, "where did that come from?"

"Who cares?" Fern said. "Just hit me with it!"

"Sure thing!" said Lester.

Splat!

This time Lester got it right and . . .

Kerblam!

Super Chicken Nugget Boy was suddenly standing before him!

"I really don't know where that came from," said Lester.

"Well, you think about it and get back to

me," said Super Chicken Nugget Boy. "In the meantime, I'm going to go out there and try to not get mashed by that meat monstrosity!"

Super Chicken Nugget Boy turned toward Massive Meatloaf Man.

"Super Chicken Nugget Boy! Thank goodness you've arrived!" Ms. Durbindin called out.

Massive Meatloaf Man screamed back! *"AAAARRRRGGGGHHHH!!!"*

"I know how you feel," Super Chicken Nugget Boy said to the meatloaf man as he carefully made his way over to Ms. Durbindin. "Sometimes all I want to do is scream too— *AH!* So, I say, go ahead, scream all you want. I'm just going to be over there by that tree where that teacher is, doing nothing particularly interesting."

Massive Meatloaf Man scratched his

head, confused, and then screamed again, *"AAAARRRRRRGGGGGHHHH!!!"* as Super Chicken Nugget Boy circled behind Ms. Durbindin's net.

"Sure, sure, let it all out," said Super Chicken Nugget Boy, in an attempt to soothe him.

"What's with all the chitchat?" Snort asked Dirk, over behind their rock. "Why doesn't Super Chicken Nugget Boy just attack him already?"

"He knows better than that," said Dirk. "If Arnie the Awesome Amphibian is no match for the meat man, there's no way that nugget is. There's no way anyone is. Except for me! Ha-ha-ha!"

"Oh, thank heavens," said Ms. Durbindin.

Massive Meatloaf Man screamed again,

with beefy bluster, *"AAAARRRRGGGG-HHHH!!!"* as he approached Super Chicken Nugget Boy and Ms. Durbindin.

"Yes," Super Chicken Nugget Boy said, looking at the meatloaf, "sometimes it feels good to scream, doesn't it? Let it out."

Super Chicken Nugget Boy grabbed the pulley and was just about to release it to lower Ms. Durbindin when he felt the massive monster's meaty hand grab him.

"Now, hold on, can we just talk about this for a second?" he said. But there was no talking whatsoever. Massive Meatloaf Man picked him up above his head and flung him fiercely.

"I knew that was too good to be true," Super Chicken Nugget Boy said to Lester, who was frighteningly close to where Super Chicken Nugget Boy had just landed.

"Don't worry," said Lester. "His meat may be red, but his brain sure isn't."

"What is that supposed to mean?" Super Chicken Nugget Boy asked.

"I don't know," said Lester. "I just thought it sounded cool and would get you inspired."

"AAAARRRRGGGGHHHH!!!"

Super Chicken Nugget Boy and Lester looked up to discover that Massive Meatloaf Man was now standing right over them.

"Mommy!!!" said Lester. "What do we do?" he asked the nugget.

Without even thinking about it, Super Chicken Nugget Boy picked Lester up and threw him at Massive Meatloaf Man's head.

Lester screamed as he collided with the meat man's fleshy face.

Super Chicken Nugget Boy sprinted back to Ms. Durbindin, jumped up, grabbed the pulley, and lowered Ms. Durbindin to the ground.

"I can't believe you threw me in Massive Meatloaf Man's face," Lester said as he got up off the ground. "He nearly snorted me up his nose."

"I had no other options," said Super Chicken Nugget Boy. "I had to distract him. It worked. It distracted him. I'm sorry. It won't happen again."

"Fine," said Lester.

Suddenly Ms. Durbindin screamed. *"AAAAAAAAHHHHH!!!"*

"AAAARRRRGGGGHHHH!!!" Massive Meatloaf Man replied.

Super Chicken Nugget Boy picked Lester up and threw him at the meatloaf's head.

Massive Meatloaf Man fell back. That was followed by the loud *snap!* of the net's pulley being activated!

SPACK!

"Well done, Super Chicken Nugget Boy!" said Ms. Durbindin.

"Yes," said Dirk, running up to the net, "well done, indeed. Thank you for doing my dirty work. Now, I'll take it from here."

"Yeah," Snort added. "From here. *Snort! Snort!*"

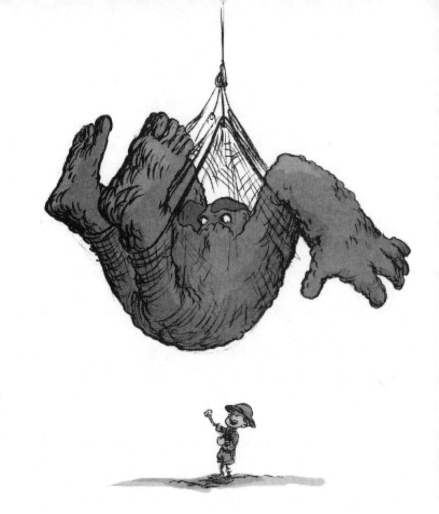

"I can't believe you threw me at his face again," said Lester, stumbling around in a daze.

12
DISPLAY AND DISMAY

It was Friday afternoon at two twenty, which meant that the students at Bert Lahr Elementary School could hardly contain themselves. Yup, you guessed it—it was time for another Display and Relay!

But this Friday the students were even more excited than usual. That's because they'd heard that Dirk Hamstone had something so amazing, so unbelievable, so terrifying, that even though he had just presented his snake that ate a porcupine the week before, he was going again this week. Kids *never* got to go two weeks in a row. But all the students wanted to see what Dirk's miraculous object was so badly that an exception was made. Also, Mrs. Hamstone told Principal Hamstone to tell Mr. Zwerkle that if he didn't let Dirk go again, he would fire him. It was those two things that convinced Mr. Zwerkle to let Dirk skip ahead of all the other kids who had things they wanted to display and go this week. But mostly it was the getting fired part.

On top of all that, the lineup was cleared so that Dirk would be the only one displaying anything, which was also unheard of.

In the audience, students guessed at what the object might be.

"Maybe it's a hairless rabbit," Janice Oglie said to Winnie Kinney and Donna Wergnort.

"Yeah, a hairless rabbit," they said.

"I hope it's a cotton candy statue of the

fifth vice president of the United States, Elbridge Gerry," Gerard Venvent said to Finneus Washington.

"I hope it's not a humongous muffin," Sissie Majors said to no one in particular. "That would be scary."

Up on the stage, behind the curtain, Dirk and Snort stood next to a giant steel box, almost entirely covered by a cloth.

"Ha-ha!" said Dirk. "In a mere matter of

moments I will become the greatest Displayer Relayer in the history of the world!"

"You sure will!" Snort said. *"Snort!"*

Just then, Fern and Lester appeared behind the curtain and walked up to Dirk.

"I really don't think this is a good idea," Fern said to Dirk.

"Are you kidding me?" Dirk said. "It's the greatest idea I've ever had!"

"No," said Lester, "I've got a bad feeling about this."

"Well, they sure don't," Dirk said, pointing out toward the audience on the other side of the curtain.

"Come on! Let's get going!" Finneus Washington shouted from his seat.

"See?" Dirk said to Lester.

"Yeah!" Farnsworth Yorb added. "I can't take the suspense for another second!"

"You hear that?" said Dirk. "That's the sound of my glory. Now, step aside. I've got a display to relay."

Fern and Lester sadly stepped away from Dirk and went to watch from the side of the stage.

Dirk looked at Snort. "What are you still doing here?"

"Um," said Snort, "I just thought . . ."

"You just thought you'd get in on some of my glory," said Dirk. "Well, think again. There's only room for one at the top of the Display and Relay Mountain. And that one is *me*! Now, beat it!"

Snort went over to stand next to Fern and Lester.

Mr. Zwerkle walked up onto the stage and stood in front of the curtain, facing the audience.

"Welcome," he said in his booming voice, "to Display and Relay!"

The kids erupted into hoots and hollers and applause like they'd never erupted into them before!

"WOOOOOOOOO!!!"

"All right," Mr. Zwerkle said. "Now, we've got a terrific team of Displayer Relayers for you today, so let's not waste any time. Our first Displayer Relayer is . . . wait, what am I saying? We have only one Displayer Relayer this week. Old habits die hard, I guess. Anyway, let's hear it for our one and only Displayer Relayer this week, *Dirk Hamstone*!"

The kids applauded like crazy for Dirk, and this time he didn't even have to glare at them to get them to do it.

The curtain went up and there was Dirk, standing next to the giant steel box, which was still covered.

"My friends," Dirk said to the audience, "once in a lifetime, if we're lucky, we are faced with something so magnificent that we couldn't even imagine it in our wildest dreams. I dare you right now. Try. Try to imagine the most captivating, horrifying, spellbinding, ferocious creature possible, and I guarantee you will not come up with anything nearly as mesmerizing and fierce as what I'm about to show you.

"So, let that be a warning to you. What I have behind this curtain is unlike anything you've ever seen in your life, in your dreams, or even in your worst *nightmares*!

"My friends, I give you . . . MASSIVE MEATLOAF MAN!"

And with that, Dirk pulled a cord, which caused the curtain to drop, which revealed

Massive Meatloaf Man standing inside a giant cage, chained to the bars.

Everyone gasped. "*Whahhh . . . ooh . . . whoa . . .*"

Massive Meatloaf Man screamed and shook the bars of the cage. "*AAAARRRRGGGG-HHHH!!!*"

All the kids in the audience screamed. "*AAAAGHHHH!*"

"Is he going to kill us?!" Winnie Kinney shouted.

"No," said Dirk, "he can't hurt you. He's locked in there behind three thousand pounds of pure steel. Look . . ."

Dirk went right up to the side of the cage.

"Hey, Meaty," he said, "you're not so tough. I've met turkey meatloaves tougher than you."

Everyone cracked up.

"*AAAARRRRGGGGHHHH!!!*" Massive

Meatloaf Man screamed, and shook his body to and fro. But it did no good. Like Dirk said, those chains and bars were pure steel, and no matter how hard he tried, Massive Meatloaf Man couldn't break them.

"Awesome!" said Allan Chen. "Just awesome!"

Everyone agreed.

"Can I get a picture with him?" Roy Clapmist called out.

"Sure!" said Dirk, "Come on up!"

"Me too?" Janice Oglie asked.

"Of course," said Dirk. "Anyone who wants to can come on up."

Within seconds, half the students at Bert Lahr Elementary School were up on the stage taking pictures with their cell phones of themselves with Massive Meatloaf Man.

"This is bad," Fern said, as he watched

his classmates and teachers treat Massive Meatloaf Man like he was some kind of meaty Mount Rushmore, taking pictures of themselves and laughing and joking with Massive Meatloaf Man in the background.

"AAAARRRRGGGGHHHH!!!" Massive Meatloaf Man roared as he grabbed the cage's bars and pulled himself close to them.

But nobody cared. They were used to his screaming by then. They just laughed. "Ha-ha-ha!"

"AAAARRRRGGGGHHHH!!!" Massive Meatloaf Man howled again, sliding his body up against the bars.

"Ha-ha-ha!" everyone laughed some more.

"AAAARRRRGGGGHHHH!!!" Massive Meatloaf Man bellowed with rage once again as he reached one of his hands through the bars.

But everyone kept laughing: "Ha-ha-ha!" as they edged a bit farther away.

Finally, Massive Meatloaf Man let out the biggest, loudest, most vicious shriek ever uttered by any massive meat product anywhere ever!

"*AAAAAAARRRRRRRGGGGGGGG-GGGGHHHHHH!!!*"

Still, everyone paid him no mind. That is, until Massive Meatloaf Man pulled off his chains and squeezed his mighty meatloaf body through the narrow spaces between the bars of the cage!

Suddenly, he was free!

"*AAAAAAGGGHHHHHH!* RUN FOR YOUR LIVES! RUN FOR YOUR LIVES!!!" screamed Donna Wergnort, which is what everyone did, except for Fern, who ran to get Arnie Simpson.

See, here's what everyone didn't know: they didn't know that while Massive Meatloaf Man looked like a tough and hard meatloaf on the outside, the real secret was that he was actually a quite soft and moist meatloaf man on the inside. Not so soft and moist that he was in danger of getting crumbly and falling apart—just soft and moist enough to slide through steel bars when he needed to.

Suddenly, the great celebration of the greatest Display and Relay ever had turned into the most horrific scene that had ever played out on the Bert Lahr Elementary School stage.

The terror was unimaginable. The chaos was beyond belief!

13
DISPLAY AND RUN AWAY!!!

The mayhem was so immense, it could be heard and felt throughout the area, even all the way over at the Gordonville Convention Center, where a very large conference just happened to be taking place.

"Goodness, what's all that ruckus?" the

convention leader said as Donna Wergnort and Gerard Venvent ran into the meeting hall shouting.

"RUN FOR YOUR LIVES! RUN FOR YOUR LIVES! THERE'S A MASSIVE MEATLOAF MAN ON THE LOOSE!"

Everyone jumped out of their seats and screamed. *"AAAAAAAHHHHHHH!!!"*

"Is this really happening?!" one man screamed.

"This must be a dream!" one woman cried out.

"I've been waiting for this moment my entire life!" shouted the convention leader.

Donna and Gerard looked at the convention leader and then looked at each other. "That's just weird," said Donna to Gerard. Gerard nodded. They then ran out to go warn more people.

So, where was Super Chicken Nugget Boy during all this time, you may ask? Good question. That's exactly the same question that Allan Chen had when he stopped Fern, as Fern was running back into the auditorium with Arnie Simpson the Salamander in his hands.

"Hey!" Allan shouted, above the screams of everyone around them. "Where's Super Chicken Nugget Boy? We need him now more than ever."

"I know," said Fern. "I'm looking for him right now."

Fern turned to run and find Lester, his ketchup connection, but right at that moment, Ms. Durbindin came running into the auditorium, knocking into Fern and sending him to the ground.

"What's going on in here?" she said as she helped Fern back up to his feet. "I heard screams and the sound of flying meat."

Fern pointed to Massive Meatloaf Man in the middle of the room, which wasn't really necessary because he was gigantic and hard to miss.

Ms. Durbindin saw him and screamed. *"YYYYAAAAAAAAHHHHHH!!!"*

Massive Meatloaf Man suddenly stopped what he was doing, which was crushing a group of fifth grade boys between his massive meat knees, and looked over to where the screaming was coming from. He would know that scream anywhere.

He took one look at Ms. Durbindin and everything changed. The ferocious look on his face transformed to a sweet, soft look of affection.

He took one step toward Ms. Durbindin.

"DON'T YOU COME ANY CLOSER!" shouted Ms. Durbindin. "I'M WARNING YOU!" And miraculously, the angry mound of meat listened and kept his distance. But then something happened that no one could've ever predicted.

A large group of people burst into the auditorium screaming. It was the same group

of people that Donna Wergnort and Gerard
Venvent had warned at the Gordonville
Convention Center, only now they all had
napkins tucked into the top of their shirts and
were carrying forks and knives.

14

FOR THE LOVE OF LOAF

"Who are you?" Fern asked the convention leader, who was standing at the front of the group.

"We're the members of the Meatloaf Lovers League," said the convention leader. "We were just having our Monthly Meatloaf Lovers League Meeting down the road. I'm the Meatloaf Lover leader. We're here to eat that meatloaf!"

"Oh, no, you are not!" said Dirk, suddenly appearing out of nowhere to stand in front of the Meatloaf Lovers. He'd been hiding under a stack of extra-large folding chairs reserved for the heavier teachers. "That meatloaf is mine!" Dirk said. "I found him! I caught him! And I'm going to make history with him!"

"Oh, no, you are not, because we're going to eat him!" said the Meatloaf Lover leader. "And we're going to do it right now."

"You're going to have to go through me first," said Dirk.

"Okay," said the Meatloaf Lover leader. "No problem."

The Meatloaf Lovers ran for the Massive Meatloaf Man with their forks and knives held high.

Dirk, who refused to step aside, was struck and launched into the air by the meatloaf-mad mob, and went whirling headfirst in Massive Meatloaf Man.

Massive Meatloaf Man, meanwhile, hadn't

been paying attention to any of what was going on between Dirk and the Meatloaf Lovers crowd because he was too busy making lovey-dovey eyes at Ms. Durbindin. Nothing gets your attention better, though, than a kid bashing into your upper thigh while an angry mob runs at you with knives and forks!

"*AAAARRRRGGGGHHHH!!!*" screamed the meaty menace.

He reached down toward Ms. Durbindin.

"No-o-o-o-o-o-o-o-o!!!" she screamed, as he grabbed her in his hand and lifted her up.

"This is seriously bad," Lester said to Fern, popping up out of a pile of meaty scraps that Massive Meatloaf Man had shed during the skirmish.

"You're telling me," Fern said, as Massive Meatloaf Man smashed through the wall of the auditorium and out onto the street.

"Ketchup time!" Fern said, as he and Lester watched Massive Meatloaf Man trudge down the street, smashing into cars and houses, and scaring people half to death . . . or even more than half to death . . . almost all the way to death . . . some people as far as nine-tenths to death.

"Oh, yeah," said Lester.

He checked his pockets.

"I can't find any," he said. "It must've got knocked loose when Massive Meatloaf Man shook me upside down. Maybe there's one buried somewhere in this meat pile. Come on, let's take a look!"

"No!" said Fern, "There's no time for looking for a ketchup in a meat-stack!"

"Then what do we do?" Lester asked.

"Follow me!" said Fern. "I've got an idea."

15
THE LOAF'S LAST STAND

Fern and Lester ran as fast as they could to catch up to the Meatloaf Lovers, who by that point had Massive Meatloaf Man surrounded right in front of the Chudnow Building—the tallest building in downtown Gordonville.

"*AAAARRRRGGGGHHHH!!!*" screamed Massive Meatloaf Man.

"*YYYYYAAAAAHHHHHH!!!*" cried Ms. Durbindin.

"All right, Meatloaf Lovers!" said the Meatloaf Lover leader. "Prepare to partake! That means EAT, if you didn't know that already."

All of the meatloaf lovers pulled out their own little packets of—what else—ketchup!

They pointed them at Massive Meatloaf Man.

"Ready!" said the Meatloaf Lover leader.

Lester, who was standing in the very back of the mob with Fern, was amazed.

"How did you know?" Lester asked.

"Aim!" said the Meatloaf Lover leader.

"Nothing goes better with meatloaf than ketchup," said Fern. "And these guys take their meatloaf seriously."

"Fire!" ordered the Meatloaf Lover leader.

At that moment, everyone squeezed their packet of ketchup, which all went sailing toward Massive Meatloaf Man. All but one, that is. That's because when the meatloaf lover at the very back of the pack squeezed his packet of ketchup, Fern jumped in front of him with Arnie.

KERBLAM!

Suddenly the Meatloaf Lover was standing in front of none other than the one and only Super Chicken Nugget Boy and Arnie the Awesome Amphibian!

The Meatloaf Lover looked at Super Chicken Nugget Boy.

"Get out of my way!" he shouted. "I'm a member of the Meatloaf Lovers League, not the Union of Chicken Nugget Nuts! I don't care about you!"

He pushed Super Chicken Nugget Boy aside so he could get up to Massive Meatloaf Man, who was now covered in ketchup and being stormed by the crazy mob!

"All right!" Super Chicken Nugget Boy said to Arnie the Awesome Amphibian. "Let's see what we can do to mop up this massive meatloaf mess!"

He took off through the crowd upon his trusty salamander, leaving Lester behind, who was more than happy to look around on the ground for any ketchup packets with little bits of ketchup left in them.

"Mm," said Lester, "all this danger is making me hungry."

Up at the front of the mob, Massive Meatloaf Man was being poked and prodded by the Meatloaf Lovers' knives and forks as they tried their hardest to pick off pieces of his melt-in-your-mouth meatiness.

Seeing that he was surrounded, Massive Meatloaf Man realized that there was no place for him to go but up. So, that's what he did.

The Meatloaf Man let out a big scream— "*AAAARRRRGGGH!!!*"—and then grabbed the side of the Chudnow Building and started pulling himself up it with Ms. Durbindin still in his hand.

"AAAHHH!!! AAAHHH!!! HELP ME!!!" screamed Ms. Durbindin, as Massive Meatloaf Man passed the building's second and third and fourth floors.

"Don't worry," Super Chicken Nugget Boy hollered up to her. "This sensational salamander and I will save you!"

Meanwhile, the Meatloaf Lovers ran into the building, hoping to grab hold of Massive Meatloaf Man through a window as he climbed up.

"That's never going to work," Super Chicken Nugget Boy said to Arnie as he guided him around to the back of the building. "The day a regular-sized person can grab a Massive Meatloaf Man off a building and pull him inside is the day I eat my own breading for lunch. Slither away, Arnie, slither away."

Arnie started slithering slyly up the back of the building with Super Chicken Nugget Boy on top of him.

"That's it, Arnie, nice and easy," said Super Chicken Nugget Boy. "We don't want to startle this freaky meaty misfit."

Massive Meatloaf Man reached the top of the Chudnow Building.

Suddenly, Super Chicken Nugget Boy and Arnie appeared on top of the building as well!

Massive Meatloaf Man turned around and

saw Super Chicken Nugget Boy and Arnie.

"Super Chicken Nugget Boy!" cried Ms. Durbindin. "Thank goodness you're here!"

Massive Meatloaf Man roared back, *"AAAAAAARRRRRRGGGGHH!!!"* and lunged at Super Chicken Nugget Boy.

Super Chicken Nugget Boy neatly side-stepped him. "Look here, Meatloaf Man," he said, "I'm not here to fight you."

Massive Meatloaf Man was about to jump at the nugget again when Ms. Durbindin shouted, "Listen to him, Meaty!"

Massive Meatloaf Man stopped and listened.

"There's no way I could defeat you in a one-on-one battle of meaty might," said Super Chicken Nugget Boy.

"Heh-heh-heh," Massive Meatloaf Man chuckled, nodding in agreement.

"I'm just here to get what's rightfully mine," said Super Chicken Nugget Boy, "and we all know what that is."

"What?" asked Ms. Durbindin.

"You," said Super Chicken Nugget Boy.

"Hrgh?" growled Massive Meatloaf Man.

"It's true," Super Chicken Nugget Boy said to the meat man. "We're in love!"

"We are?" said Ms. Durbindin.

Super Chicken Nugget Boy winked at Ms. Durbindin.

"Of course we are. Don't try to deny it, Celia," he said, calling her by her first name.

"Oh yeah," she said. "Now I remember. Super Chicken Nugget Boy and I are madly in love."

"*AAAAARRRRRRGGGGGGHHH!!!*" screamed Massive Meatloaf Man.

"I know it's hard to hear," said Super

Chicken Nugget Boy. "It's never easy to hear that the person who you love doesn't love you back, but those are the facts. So, if you'll just give her to me, we can get this whole nonsense over with and we'll be on our way."

"Yeah," said Ms. Durbindin, "and don't worry, I'm sure there's someone nice out there for you too. Maybe a cute meaty burger babe."

Massive Meatloaf Man wailed in despair, *"AAAAARRRRRRGGGGGGHH!!!"*

"You don't like burger babes?" said Ms. Durbindin. "Then maybe a lovely little lady steak."

That did it! Massive Meatloaf Man threw his arms up in the air and waved them around like a maniac, shaking Ms. Durbindin to and fro.

"Come on, Meatloaf," said Super Chicken

Nugget Boy. "Just give me the teacher!"

But there was no way that was going to happen. Massive Meatloaf Man was too upset, too furious, and too heartbroken to do anything like that.

Just then, the doors of the roof were flung open!

Everyone looked over.

"IT'S THE MEATLOAF LOVERS!" shouted Super Chicken Nugget Boy.

Knives and forks in hand, the Meatloaf Lovers League minions descended upon the meaty maniac.

At the same time, a large shadow came over the entire roof.

Everyone looked up.

It was Dirk Hamstone, holding a giant net out of the door of a hovering helicopter!

"You're mine now, Mr. Meat Monster!" shouted Dirk.

"It doesn't look good for you," Super Chicken Nugget Boy said to Massive Meatloaf Man.

Massive Meatloaf Man screamed.

"AAAAARRRRRRGGGGGGHH!!!"

"Come on, give me the woman! We belong together!" said Super Chicken Nugget Boy, with the Meatloaf Lovers getting closer and Dirk up above adjusting his net, preparing to strike.

Massive Meatloaf Man looked all around, shook his head, and let out a pitiful howl. "AAAWWWOOOOOOOOOOOO!!!"

He started running toward the edge of the building.

"No-o-o-o-o-o-o-o-o-o-o!!!" screamed Super Chicken Nugget Boy.

Massive Meatloaf Man lifted one leg to the edge of the building and was about to jump when Ms. Durbindin shouted out, "I don't know what I'll do if I never get to see my nugget again!"

Hearing that was just too much for the

meatloaf; he stopped in his tracks, bent over, and gently placed Ms. Durbindin down on the roof.

"*AAAAAAHHHHHHH!!!*" screamed the Meatloaf Lovers as they were just about to dig in to the Massive Meatloaf Man.

"Ha-ha!" screamed Dirk as he dropped his net down right at that moment over Massive Meatloaf Man's head.

But it wasn't meant to be. Just as the net dropped and the Meatloaf Lovers were reaching their magnificent meal, Massive Meatloaf Man took a giant leap off the roof of the Chudnow Building and went soaring through the air.

If you've never been witness to a Massive Meatloaf Man soaring through the air, well then all you need to know is that it's a magical moment . . . that is, to everyone besides

every member of the Meatloaf Lovers League, who were now caught in the net that Dirk had intended for the Massive Meatloaf Man. To them, it was the greatest of great disappointments. Dirk wasn't happy about it either.

"Ha! He's in the factory!" screamed Dirk.

"We can still get him!" shouted the Meatloaf Lovers leader.

"YAY!" yelled the Meatloaf Lovers.

But they didn't stand a chance. Moments after the Massive Meatloaf Man landed inside the factory, he barreled back out through the front door. The next thing anyone knew, he was

running down the streets of Gordonville, pajamas clinging to all sorts of parts of his body, as he hightailed it back to the Burkeburkes where he belonged.

Up on the roof of the Chudnow Building, Ms. Durbindin turned to thank Super Chicken Nugget Boy for what he had done. But she'd have to wait. He was gone, just like that. She did, however, find Fern and Arnie Simpson the Salamander up there.

"Are you all right?" Fern asked, approaching Ms. Durbindin.

"Goodness, Fernando, what in heavens are you doing up here?" she asked.

"Arnie and I just wanted to come up and make sure you were okay," Fern said, handing her the salamander.

"Oh, my, Arnie, you came too!" said Ms. Durbindin, as Arnie bit off a little piece of meatloaf that was stuck to her elbow. "Isn't that sweet?"

Then she broke down crying, overwhelmed, as Arnie nibbled on the meatloaf and thought to himself, Mm . . . really quite tasty.

16

JUST ANOTHER DAY AT THE BEA—

"Yes! Yes! Yes!" Lester said. "Nothing like the beach to calm a man's mood and refresh his spirit!"

"You said it!" said Fern. "Boogie boarding! Beach volleyball! Sand castles! And suntan lotion launch contests!"

Fern and Lester were taking the day to get away from all of the Bert Lahr lunacy and crime-fighting chaos and live it up a little.

"And best of all," said Fern, as they entered Gordonville's Borgwardt Beach, "no monsters!"

"No beasts!" added Lester.

"No meaty mental cases!" said Fern.

"No lousy loaf temper tantrums!" said Lester. "Just peace . . ."

"And quiet . . ." said Fern.

Suddenly they heard Roy Clapmist's voice, calling out. "Oh, my!"

They turned to look. He was out in the water, his body jerking back and forth.

"What the—?" he said. Then he was still.

"Oh, I guess it was noth . . ."

His body shook!

"YIKES! HEY, WHAT'S DOWN THERE?"

His body quaked like crazy!

"He's still terrible at this," Lester said to Fern. "Totally not believable, and he's even really in the water. He needs some serious Help, I'm Being Eaten by a Shark lessons from me."

"*AAHH!!!*" Roy screamed. "*AAHH!! Somebody please h—*"

He ducked his head down and flung his arms up above it.

"*Glug, glug, glug.*"

He threw his head up again.

"I can't . . ."

"This has to be the worst Help, I'm Being Eaten by a Shark I've ever seen," Lester said. "Okay, Roy! You can stop now! We get it!"

But Roy didn't stop. He ducked his head back down and shook around.

"Give it up, Roy!" shouted Lester.

"I don't think he's joking," Fern said.

Roy popped his head up and flung his arms all around like a madman.

"*AAGHH!* HELP! I'M BEING EATEN BY A . . ."

Before Roy could get the words out, a giant

beast leaped up from the water with Roy in its mouth.

Fern and Lester screamed. "TITANIC TUNA FISH SALAD SHARK!"

Yes, it's true! Roy was not only really and truly being attacked by a shark, but it was the one and only incredibly rare and most deadly of all sharks—the dreaded Titanic Tuna Fish Salad Shark!

"So much for suntan-lotion launches," said Lester.

"A nugget's work is never done!" said Fern, and with that, Lester squirted Fern with a premium packet of ketchup that he'd been saving especially for a delectable Borgwardt Beach Snack Shac onion ring rack!

Kerblam!

In an instant, Fern went from simple fourth grade beach bum to colossal coastal crusader!

"DON'T WORRY!" Super Chicken Nugget Boy called out, as he ran toward the water. "MY BREADING IS BUOYANT, AND MY FEARLESSNESS FLOATS! I'LL CAN THAT TITANIC TUNA FISH SALAD SHARK, AND YOUR BUDDIES WILL BE BACK BURYING YOU IN THE SAND IN NO TIME! UNLESS YOU DON'T LIKE DOING THAT BECAUSE YOU GET SAND UP YOUR BATHING SUIT, WHICH CAN BE UNPLEASANT AND UNCOMFORTABLE! EITHER WAY, I'M COMING TO SAVE YOU!"

Super Chicken Nugget Boy dived into the water, and just like that he was back exactly where he belonged, whether on land or in the sea, mincing meat and foiling fishies and keeping the world safe from food-related freaks now and forever!